This book belongs to

Cameron Elizabeth Frend

Aesop's Fables

RETOLD BY

Fiona Black

ILLUSTRATED BY

Richard Bernal

ARIEL BOOKS

ANDREWS AND McMEEL

KANSAS CITY

Library of Congress Cataloging-in-Publication Data

Black, Fiona.
    Aesop's fables / retold by Fiona Black ; illustrated by Richard Bernal.
        p.   cm.
    Summary: A collection of fables retold from Aesop, including "The
Hare and the Tortoise," "The Ant and the Grasshopper," and "Androcles
and the Lion."
    ISBN 0–8362–4914–3 : $6.95
    1. Fables. [1. Fables.] I. Aesop. II. Bernal, Richard, ill. III. Title.
PZ8.2.B58   Ae   1991
398.2—dc20   91–11923
[E]   CIP
                                                                  AC

Design: Susan Hood and Mike Hortens
Art Direction: Armand Eisen, Mike Hortens, and Julie Phillips
Art Production: Lynn Wine
Production: Julie Miller and Lisa Shadid

Aesop's Fables

The Hare and the Tortoise

A hare was always making fun of a tortoise for being so slow. "Get moving, slowpoke," he would shout. "Is that the fastest you can go?" One day, the tortoise decided that he had had enough and challenged the hare to a race.

The hare laughed and laughed. "A race with you?" he scoffed. "I'll get to the finish before you even cross the starting line!"

"Never mind that," said the tortoise. "Let's just have the race."

A course was set by all the animals and the fox was to be the judge. When the fox barked, the race began.

Quicker than you can say "Go," the hare sprang ahead and vanished down the path. Meanwhile the tortoise went along at his usual slow speed.

Before long, the hare decided to stop and have a rest. "After all," he thought, "that slow tortoise will take hours to catch up with me!"

So he stretched out on some shady grass. Soon he began to yawn. "Perhaps I'll just take a quick nap," he said, and with that, he fell asleep.

Meanwhile the tortoise kept plodding along. And when the hare awoke, the tortoise was at the finish line.

So the moral of the story is as follows: In the end, slow and steady wins the race.

The Fox and the Grapes

A hungry fox was walking one day when he
saw some ripe grapes hanging from a vine.
The fox leaped up for the nearest bunch and
snapped his jaws, but he missed. He tried
again and again, but the grapes were just out
of reach. At last, he slunk off, muttering, "I
never wanted those grapes, anyway. They are
probably sour!"

This story teaches us that it is all too easy
to scorn the things we cannot have.

The Goose with the Golden Eggs

One day a farmer discovered that his goose had laid a pure gold egg. Every day after that the goose laid another golden egg. The farmer grew rich, but he also grew greedy. "If I kill the goose," he thought, "I can get all her treasure at once!" So he cut the bird open—and found nothing!

And so we learn that by trying to get more, the greedy sometimes lose all!

THE MILKMAID
AND HER PAIL

One day a milkmaid was walking to market with a bucket of milk on her head. As she walked she thought of what she would do with the money she would get for her milk.

"I shall buy some hens," she said to herself happily, "and they will lay an egg each a day. These I will sell to the pastor's wife, and with that money I will buy myself a new dress and a new ribbon for my hair. They shall be emerald green, for that is the color that suits me best. Then in my new clothes, I will go to the fair."

At the thought of those new clothes, the milkmaid exclaimed, "I will look so pretty that all the young men will ask me to dance. But I will just toss my head at them—like this!"

But when she tossed her head, down fell the pail! The milk spilled onto the ground, and with it went the milkmaid's happy day-dreams. All she would get now was a scolding when she returned home.

And this is why we must always remember never to count our chickens until they are hatched!

The Wolf in Sheep's Clothing

A wolf had been prowling around a flock of sheep for several days. But the shepherd guarded his sheep so well that the wolf was growing hungry and desperate.

One day, the wolf came upon a sheepskin that the shepherd had thrown away. The wolf pulled the skin on over its own coat and mingled with the flock. Even the watchful shepherd was fooled.

That evening, the hungry shepherd went to the fold and seized the first animal he saw to kill for his supper. But it was the wolf he chose, mistaking it for a sheep. And so the wolf's clever disguise cost him his life.

By this story we learn that tricksters are often caught by their own tricks.

THE COUNTRY MOUSE
AND THE CITY MOUSE

Once a country mouse invited a friend from
town to pay him a visit. Now the country
mouse lived simply, but in honor of his
friend, he brought out every last morsel
of food he had—peas and barley, nuts and
berries.

The town mouse turned up his nose at
this plain country fare. "How can you bear
to live like this?" he said. "Come to the city
and I will show you how fine and exciting
life can be."

So the country mouse agreed to go to town with his friend. Soon they arrived at the great house where the town mouse lived. There, in the dining room, they found the remains of a splendid feast. The two friends gorged themselves on fine biscuits and cakes, imported cheeses, exotic fruits, and all sorts of other delicacies. "My friend was right," thought the country mouse. "City life is quite fine!"

Suddenly there was a horrible noise. "What is that?" squeaked the country mouse.

"Oh," replied the town mouse, "that is only the master's dogs!"

At that, the door burst open, and several people entered the room, followed by two huge dogs. The mice quickly scurried off the table and hid in the fireplace.

At last, when all was quiet again, the country mouse crept from his hiding place. "I am going home!" he whispered to his friend. "Town life is exciting, but I prefer my quiet life in the country. I'd rather eat my simple fare in peace than feast in fear and trembling."

And that is the lesson of this story.

The Ant
and the Grasshopper

One cold autumn day, an ant was storing the wheat she had gathered for winter, when along came a grasshopper begging for food.

"What did you do all summer?" asked the ant. "I sang!" was the reply.

"As you sang all summer," said the ant, "you can dance all winter!"

So don't forget: one must always prepare today for the needs of tomorrow.

The Oak and the Reed

A mighty oak tree grew by a river. One day a fierce storm knocked the tree down. After the storm ended, the oak tree was amazed to see the river reeds still standing, and he asked them how this was possible.

"It is simple," one reed replied. "When the wind came, you were too proud to bend even a little. But I know I am only a humble reed. So when the wind blew, I bent over. That is why I am still here."

And so we learn that it is better to bend than to break.

Androcles and the Lion

There once was a slave named Androcles whose master treated him cruelly. Androcles could bear it no longer, and one day he ran away into the forest. There he came upon a roaring lion. At first he was frightened, but then he saw that the lion was crying from pain.

As Androcles drew near, the lion put out its paw. Androcles saw a large thorn in one of the lion's toes and pulled it out.

The lion was so grateful, it licked Androcles' hand and led him to its cave. Androcles remained with the lion for some time, and every day the lion caught game for them to eat.

One day, as Androcles and the lion were hunting together, they were both captured. They were taken to the city and put in a circus. For entertainment, Androcles was to be thrown to a lion that had not been fed for several days to make it as fierce and hungry as possible. The emperor himself was coming to watch the show.

On the day of the event, Androcles was led to the center of the arena. Then the lion was let out of its cage. With a terrible roar, it bounded toward the poor slave.

As the snarling lion drew near Androcles, it suddenly stopped, rolled over, and licked his hand. The emperor was so impressed by the unusual sight that he called Androcles before him to explain. When Androcles told the emperor the whole story, the emperor set him free. He also set the lion free to return to the forest.

And so this story teaches us that a good deed never goes unrewarded.

The Fox and the Crow

Once a crow stole a piece of cheese and flew to a treetop to enjoy her prize. A fox caught sight of her, and thought to himself, "If I am clever and act quickly, I shall have that cheese for my supper!"

So he sat under the tree and began to speak to the crow in his softest and most polite tone of voice. "Good day, Mistress Crow," he began. "How fine you look today! Your feathers are so glossy and black, and your claws look so strong.

"Why, you look like a queen perched there on that branch," the fox crooned. "I only wish that I could hear your voice, for I am certain that it must be every bit as beautiful as the rest of you!"

The vain crow was delighted, for she believed his every word. She nodded her head and flapped her wings with joy. She was especially pleased that the fox had praised her voice, for she had often been told that her caw was rather harsh. So, thinking to impress the fox with her lovely voice, she opened her beak wide.

Down fell the cheese right into the fox's open jaws! As the fox trotted away, licking his lips, he called to the crow, "Next time someone flatters you, you would do well to be more cautious!"

And so we learn from the tale of the fox and the crow that flatterers are not to be trusted!

THE LION AND THE MOUSE

One day, a lion was sleeping in his den when a naughty mouse scampered across his nose. This woke the lion up and made him cross. He swung at the mouse and trapped him under his paw. He was about to kill him, when the mouse squeaked, "Please forgive me, your majesty. Don't kill me. If you spare me, I promise that one day I will do you a good turn to repay your kindness." Amused at the idea of a mouse helping him, the king of beasts let his prisoner go.

Some time later when the lion was in the forest, he became trapped in a net. The lion roared as loudly as he could. The mouse heard him and recognized his voice. He ran to his friend to find him tangled in the net's ropes.

"Good day, your majesty," the mouse said. "I know you laughed when I said I would repay your kindness to me, but now my chance has come."

Then the mouse began to gnaw at the ropes with his sharp little teeth. It was not long before he had gnawed through the ropes and the lion was able to escape the trap.

The lesson this story teaches us is simple: no kind act, however small, is ever wasted.

The Mouse Council

For many years the mice who inhabited a certain house lived in fear of the household pet, the cat. One day, they called a meeting to decide what should be done. Many suggestions were made, but none of them was suitable. At last, a young mouse, looking very serious and important, stood up and addressed the group.

"I propose that we hang a bell around the cat's neck," the young mouse declared. "That way we will always know when she is coming and be able to escape!"

The mice clapped and cheered. The young mouse's plan seemed the perfect solution.

Then an old mouse stood up and said, "The young mouse's plan is clever. But tell me, which one of us will bell the cat?"

And the mice learned, it is one thing to propose a plan and quite another to carry it out!

The Boy Who Cried Wolf

A shepherd boy grew weary of passing his days alone in the pasture with his sheep. One day, to stir up some excitement, he shouted, "Wolf! Wolf!" All the villagers came running with sticks and clubs. The trick worked so well, that the boy tried it again and again. One day a real wolf came. The boy called for help, but this time no one came, and the wolf ate all his sheep.

The moral of the story is that liars are not believed even when they tell the truth!